FRANKLIN PARK PUBLIC LIBRARY
FRANKLIN PARK, IL.

For James.

We have your balloons, Grandpa—J. O.

For Mom and Dad—D. W.

SIMON & SCHUSTER BOOKS FOR YOUNG READERS

An imprint of Simon & Schuster Children's Publishing Division

1230 Avenue of the Americas, New York, New York 10020

Text copyright © 2018 by Jessie Oliveros

Illustrations copyright © 2018 by Dana Wulfekotte

All rights reserved, including the right of reproduction in whole or in part in any form.

SIMON & SCHUSTER BOOKS FOR YOUNG READERS is a trademark of Simon & Schuster, Inc.

For information about special discounts for bulk purchases, please contact

Simon & Schuster Special Sales at 1-866-506-1949 or business@simonandschuster.com.

The Simon & Schuster Speakers Bureau can bring authors to your live event. For more information or

to book an event, contact the Simon & Schuster Speakers Bureau at 1-866-248-3049 or

visit our website at www.simonspeakers.com.

Book design by Lucy Ruth Cummins

The text for this book was set in Quimbly.

The illustrations for this book were rendered in pencil, colored pencil, ink, gouache, and Photoshop.

Manufactured in China

0618 SCP

First Edition

2 4 6 8 10 9 7 5 3 1

Library of Congress Cataloging-in-Publication Data

Names: Oliveros, Jessie, author. | Wulfekotte, Dana, illustrator.

Title: The remember balloons / Jessie Oliveros ; illustrated by Dana Wulfekotte.

Description: New York : Simon & Schuster Books for Young Readers, [2018] |

Summary: James has a bunch of balloons, each of which holds a special memory, but as his grandfather

ages and loses his own balloons, James discovers that he is gaining new ones.

Identifiers: LCCN 2016047186| ISBN 9781481489157 (hardcover : alk. paper) | ISBN 9781481489164 (ebook)

Subjects: | CYAC: Memory—Fiction. | Old age—Fiction. | Family life—Fiction. | Balloons—Fiction.

Classification: LCC PZ7.1.O47 Rem 2018 | DDC [E]—dc23 LC record available at https://lccn.loc.gov/2016047186

the remember balloons

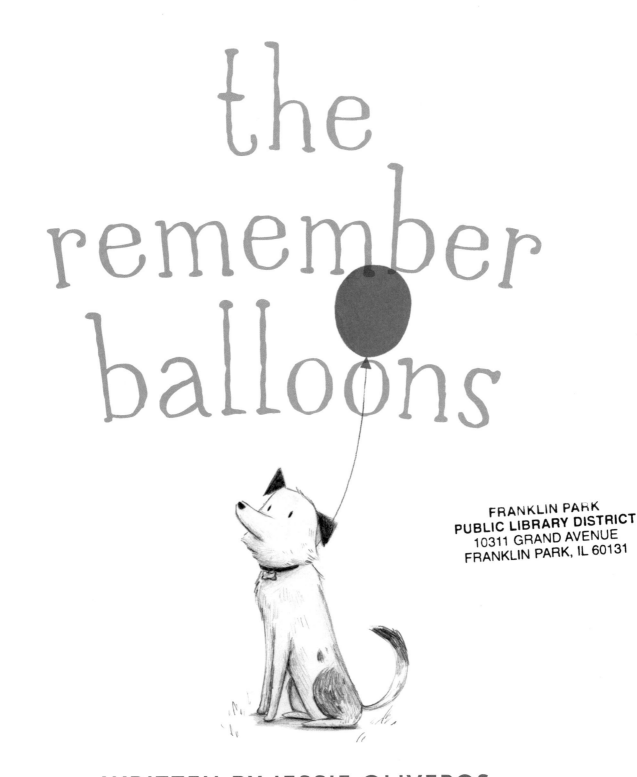

WRITTEN BY JESSIE OLIVEROS
ILLUSTRATED BY DANA WULFEKOTTE

Simon & Schuster Books for Young Readers

New York   London   Toronto   Sydney   New Delhi

$\mathcal{I}$ have lots and lots of balloons,
way more than my little brother.

"This one's my favorite," I tell him,
pointing to the balloon filled with
my last birthday party.

When I look at it, I can see the pony again.

I can still taste the chocolate frosting.

Mom and Dad have
more balloons than I do.

Grandpa has lived so long,
he has more balloons than all of us together!
And the stories he has inside those balloons?

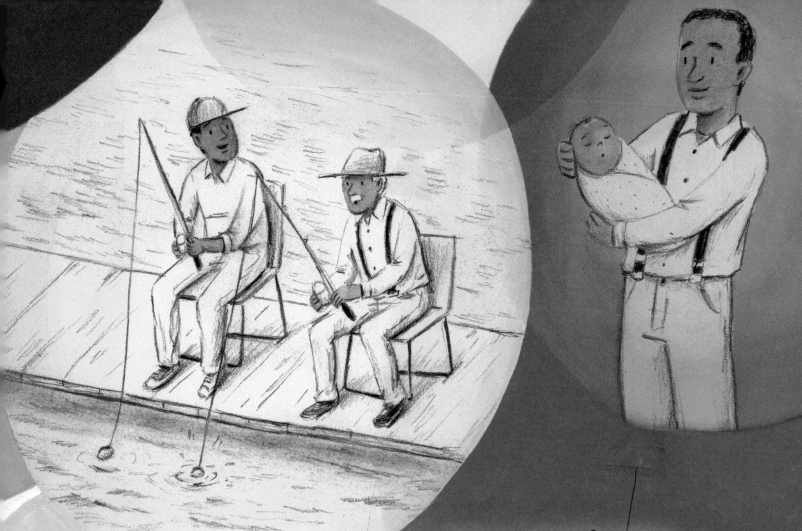

They're better than ponies and chocolate frosting.

"What's in your
yellow balloon?"
I ask him.

Grandpa's eyes light up.
"We'd just come back from picking
blackberries along the muddy banks of the creek.
Our berry-splattered faces gave Aunt Nelle's cow such
a fright, she didn't make milk for days."

"What about that blue one, Grandpa?"

"That's the time I lost my favorite dog, Jack." Grandpa chuckles. "I found him chasing butterflies next to the schoolhouse. Only Jack could get me to school on a Saturday!"

"And that one?" I point to a purple balloon above his head. Grandpa looks up and smiles, his face alive with remembering.

"That's the day I married your grandma in the little church on Cedar Lane. We danced that night under the stars, and oh—how I loved her!"

I don't have to ask him about the silver balloon, because I have one too.

That was the day we stood on the dock till the sun went down, feeling tug after tug on our lines. Grandpa and I must have caught a thousand fish.

Grandpa ruffles my hair like he always does.

"That's one of my favorite balloons."

"Mine, too," I say.

But Grandpa has been having problems with his balloons lately. One will get caught in a tree, and he'll tell me the same story over and over.

"Let me tell you about the Christmas I went to Aunt Nelle's farm," Grandpa says, even though he just finished telling me about it.

Other times, a balloon will float right out of his hand,

and he won't even know it.

"It's okay, Grandpa!"
I yell as I run after it.

Every time I almost reach it,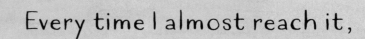

but it always slips away.

"Something's wrong with Grandpa," I tell my parents.
"He can't hold on to his balloons anymore."

Mom looks at me with sad eyes. "That happens sometimes. When people grow older."

Grandpa's balloons start floating away faster and faster.
   Running down streets and up hills, I watch the balloons grow smaller.

He finally loses
the silver one.

I watch it float away until
I can't see it anymore.

"Why did you
let it go?"
I yell.
"That was
our balloon!"

Then I sit on the sidewalk and cry.

I feel Grandpa pat my back, but he doesn't ruffle my hair like he always did. "Why are you crying, child? There's nothing to cry about."

One day, I go to see him,
and all his balloons are gone.

"Grandpa?" I say, but he
doesn't look at me.

"It'll be okay,"
Dad says. "Look up!"

I have new balloons now. A yellow
one filled with blackberries and a
cow. A blue one filled with Grandpa
and his favorite dog. A purple one
filled with a wedding day. . . .

"See?" Mom says.
"Now they're yours to share."

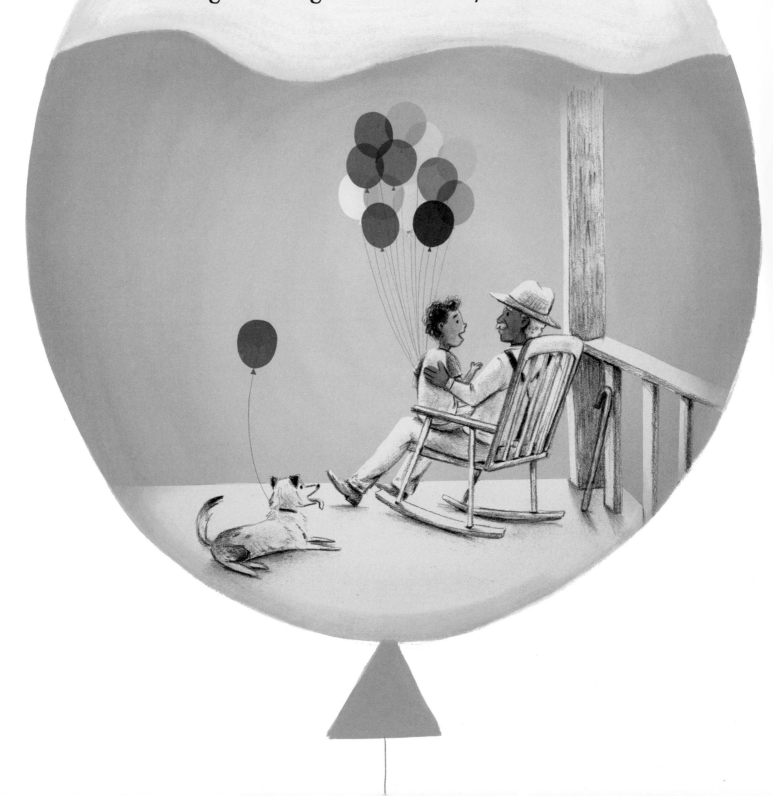

So I climb into Grandpa's lap
and begin telling him about my new balloons.